The Berenstain Bears

FIRST TIME BOOKS®

- New Baby
- Go to School
- Go to the Doctor
- Moving Day
- The Sitter
- Visit the Dentist
- Go to Camp
- Get in a Fight
- In the Dark
- The Messy Room
- Trouble with Money
- The Truth
- Too Much TV
- Mama's New Job
- Meet Santa Bear
- Too Much Junk Food
- Forget Their Manners
- Learn About Strangers
- No Girls Allowed
- Too Much Birthday
- Get Stage Fright
- The Week at Grandma's
- Go Out for the Team
- Trouble with Friends
- The Bad Habit
- Blaze a Trail
- The Big Road Race
- The Missing Honey
- On the Job
- Trouble at School
- The Bad Dream
- The Double Dare

- Get the Gimmies
- The Ghost of the Forest
- Ready, Get Set, Go!
- The In-Crowd
- Too Much Vacation
- Trick or Treat
- The Slumber Party
- The Prize Pumpkin
- Trouble with Pets
- Don't Pollute (Anymore)
- The Trouble with Grownups
- Too Much Pressure
- The Bully
- The New Neighbors
- The Green-Eyed Monster
- Too Much Teasing
- Count Their Blessings
- The Homework Hassle
- The Blame Game
- Get Their Kicks
- Lend a Helping Hand
- Mad, Mad, Mad Toy Craze
- Think of Those in Need
- The Big Question
- The Birds, the Bees, and the Berenstain Bears
- Baby Makes Five
- The Big Blooper
- Dollars and Sense
- The Excuse Note
- The Real Easter Eggs
- Report Card Trouble

The Berenstain Bears

BIGGER BOOK OF STORIES

The Berenstain Bears

BIGGER BOOK
OF STORIES

STAN & JAN BERENSTAIN

CHILDREN'S BOOK-OF-THE-MONTH CLUB
NEW YORK

The Berenstain Bears
BIGGER BOOK OF STORIES

The Berenstain Bears
BIGGER BOOK
OF STORIES

The Berenstain Bears
Go to School

When summertime ends
and the weather turns cool,
most little bears
are ready for school....

It had been a wonderful summer for the
Bear family. They had gone swimming and boating
at the lake. They had picnicked in the woods, and
taken many walks along sunny paths.

But now summer was just about over. There was a nip in the air. The birds were beginning to fly south, and the leaves on the tree house were changing colors.

One evening at supper, Brother Bear said, "I'm getting tired of summer vacation. I think I'm ready to go back to school!"

"That *is* good news," said Papa Bear. "Because school will be starting again, very soon!"

Sister Bear's ears perked up at the word *school*.

Mama Bear noticed. "As a matter of fact," she said, "Sister and I are going to meet her new teacher tomorrow."

This year Sister would be starting kindergarten. And she wasn't quite sure how she felt about it.

She liked being at home
with her mother and father...

her books and toys...

and all her friends.

"What will school be like, Mama?" she asked
at bedtime.

"You'll find out tomorrow," said Mama as she
tucked Sister in and kissed her good-night.

The next day, Mama and Sister
packed a lunch and took the long
walk down the winding dirt road
to the Bear Country School.

Handybear Gus was up on a ladder, fixing the roof.
"Hello!" said Mama. "This is Sister Bear.
She starts kindergarten next week."
"We'll be glad to have her," said Gus.
"Miss Honeybear is the kindergarten teacher.
You'll find her inside."

"Hello there!" said Miss Honeybear in a loud, jolly voice. "Come right in and look around!"

Sister thought Miss Honeybear's voice was a little scary. But she let Miss Honeybear take her hand and lead her into the kindergarten room.

What a big friendly room! It had yellow
curtains and tables and chairs that looked
just right for someone Sister's size.

"What do you *do* in kindergarten?"
Sister asked as they sat down for lunch.
"We read stories, sing songs, learn our
ABCs, paint pictures, play games, make things
out of clay, build with blocks—we do *lots*
of things!" said Miss Honeybear.

Those were all things Sister liked to do.
And she had never seen such big jars of paint...
or such fine blocks. There was even a whole
barrel of clay....

School might be fun, after all, thought Sister
by the time she and Mama started home.

But when the big morning came,
Sister began to worry again.
"Mama!" she said. "What if I
don't like school? What if I just
don't like it?"

Just then the big yellow school bus
pulled up to the tree house.

"Stop worrying!" said Brother Bear.
"School is fun. You'll like it. Now
let's get going or we'll miss the bus!"

He grabbed her hand and away they went.

Every so often the bus stopped and more bears climbed on.

Most of them were excited like Brother. But some of the smaller ones were quiet like Sister.

As more and more old friends climbed on, they got noisier and noisier . . .and the smaller ones got quieter.

The little bear who sat
next to Sister began to look
worried, so she smiled
at him and held his hand.

Apple

At last the bus arrived. The Bear Country School looked very nice. Handybear Gus had fixed the roof, and painted the trim, and cut the grass.

And Miss Honeybear's kindergarten room looked beautiful. Everything was ready!

Before very long, the kindergartners got noisy! Two of them wanted to play with the same dump truck. Two others wanted to look at the same book. And a whole gang of them wanted to be first to play with the blocks. What a commotion!

Suddenly a loud, jolly voice called out: "STORY TIME!" Miss Honeybear was calling the class to the book corner. *That* quieted things down.

After the story, Sister tried
everything. She painted a picture. . .

helped build a block city. . .

made a giant clay doughnut. . .

and looked at the books.

She ate all of her bread and
honey at snack time. . .

and she fell asleep
at nap time.

When she climbed off the bus
with Brother at the end of the day,
Sister was the excited one.

"Mama! Papa! Look what I did
in school today!" she said, holding
up her painting.

A few days later, the weather turned warm again, as it sometimes does in early fall.

Brother was restless at breakfast. "I wish it was still summer vacation," he said, "so I wouldn't have to go to school today."

"Oh, come on, Brother Bear!" said Sister. "School is fun. Let's get going or we'll miss the bus!"

On the bus, all the bears were talking about the things they were going to do at school—soccer practice, science projects, music lessons—all kinds of things!

H-m-m, thought Brother. Sister Bear was right. School *is* fun!

And off they went in the big yellow bus
to the Bear Country School.

The Berenstain Bears
VISIT THE DENTIST

Taking good care of their teeth
Is something all bears do.
That's why Sis and Brother brush—
And go to the dentist, too.

A FIRST TIME BOOK®

One morning, Sister Bear woke up in the same old bed, in the same old pajamas, and yawned the same old yawn. But something was different.

"I have a looth tooth," she told Brother Bear.

"Well, push it back and forth with your tongue, and maybe it'll come out," yawned Brother, as he turned over to go back to sleep.

"Then what?" asked Sister. Brother had told her about the tooth fairy, and she wanted to hear it again.

"Then, put it under your pillow, and the tooth fairy will take it away and leave a new coin in its place. . . ."

"But," Brother added, "be sure to tell Mama about it first!"

Later, at breakfast, when Mama was reminding Brother that he had a dentist's appointment after school, she noticed that Sister was eating funny.

"She has a loose tooth," Brother explained.

"When it comth out," said Sister, wiggling it with her tongue, "I'm going to put it under my pillow for the tooth fairy."

"If she doesn't wiggle it out, she can come to the dentist with us and he can *yank* it out!" Brother grinned.

"Never mind that kind of talk," said Mama. "Dr. Bearson doesn't yank. He's very gentle and very careful."

"I'll get it out myself, Thmartie!" Sister shouted, as Brother hopped onto the big yellow school bus.

But Sister was still wiggling her loose tooth with her tongue when she and Mama met Brother after school and went to the dentist.

"Ith thtill thtuck," she said, showing
Dr. Bearson her loose tooth.

"Well," said the dentist, "I'll have a look
at it after I examine Brother's teeth. You can
stand on this stool and watch—if that's all
right with Brother."

"Sure," said Brother, as he climbed into the
special cub's seat in the big dentist's chair.
"She can watch me and see how it's done."

Brother had been to the dentist before, and
he couldn't help showing off just a little.

Sister watched as Dr. Bearson checked
each one of Brother's teeth with a
special little tool.
"How do you see the backs?" she asked.

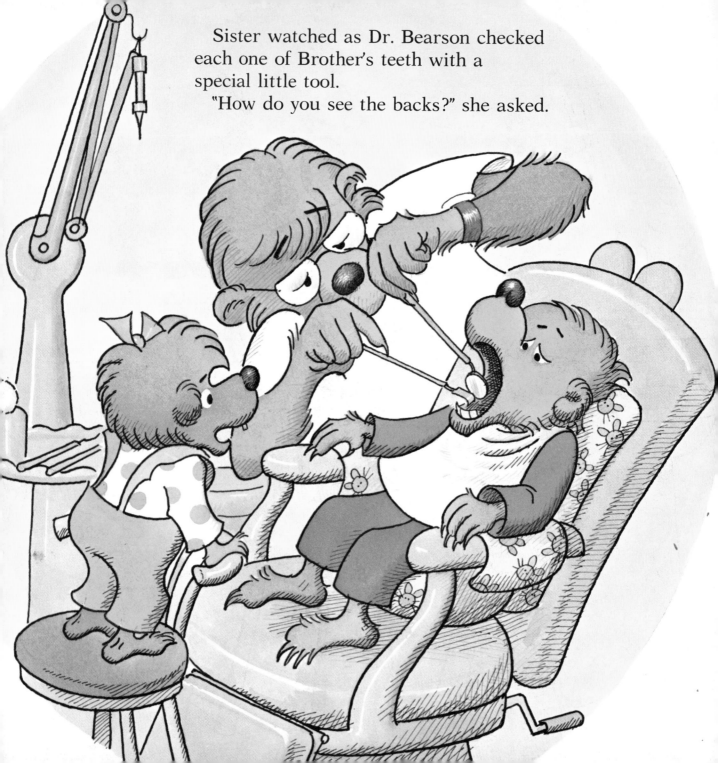

"With this little mirror,"
said the dentist. "Here. Have
a look."

"Wow!" said Sister, looking into
Brother Bear's mouth. "It looks like
a cave. A cave with a tongue!"

While Dr. Bearson checked
Brother Bear's teeth, Sister
looked at the other tools on his
work tray—there were . . .

little picks, a scraper . . .

a tamper, and . . .

ULP!—a yanker!

She had become so interested
that she had forgotten all about
her loose tooth! She went to work
wiggling again. She wiggled hard.
But it was still stuck.

There were some other interesting
dentist's things:

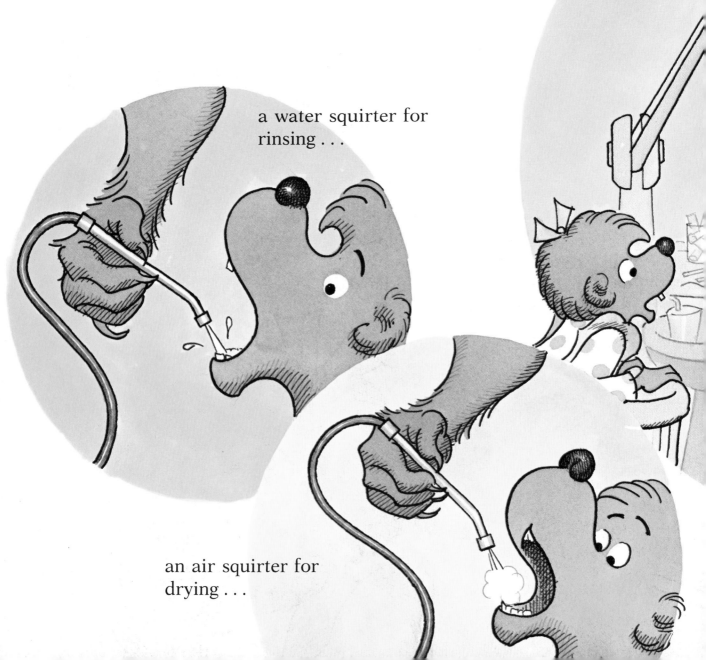

a water squirter for
rinsing . . .

an air squirter for
drying . . .

and a little drill on the end of a big hinged arm for cleaning out a cavity. And Brother had a cavity!

"It's just a tiny one," said Dr. Bearson, "in the last of your baby molars. But it's best to fill it to keep it from getting bigger."

"Ummm," said Brother, bravely.

I'm glad it's not me, thought Sister—still wiggling.

After Dr. Bearson cleaned out the cavity,
he rinsed it with the water squirter and
dried it with the air squirter.

Then he mixed up some
filling cement . . .

and filled it.

He gently tamped the filling
down and scraped it smooth.
A final rinse, and Brother jumped
down—as good as new.

"Your turn!" he said.

Bravely, Sister climbed
up into the cub's seat—
still wiggling, but that
loose tooth just didn't
seem to want to come out.

"Hmmm," said the dentist, looking at the tooth.

"Ulp!" said Sister, waiting for him to reach for those big yankers. But while she waited, Dr. Bearson gripped the tooth with a piece of gauze, gave a tug, and . . .

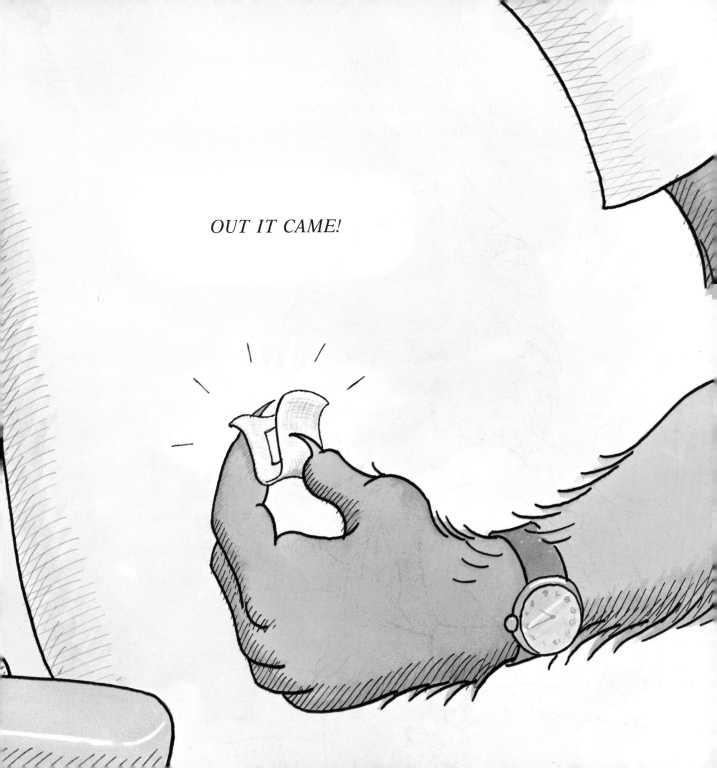

Sister looked at the tooth. It was very tiny. Dr. Bearson gave it to her to keep. Now it was her turn to hop down as good as new.

"Don't I get a lollipop or something for being good?" she asked Brother.

"You get a balloon," he said. "Lollipops aren't good for your teeth."

The next morning, Sister plunged her hand under her pillow and found a shiny new dime where the tooth had been.

"The tooth fairy came!" she told Brother.

"I told you she would," he yawned.

Then she ran into the next room to show Mama her shiny new dime.

The Berenstain Bears
and
THE TRUTH

No matter how you hope,
No matter how you try,
You can't make truth
Out of a lie.

The Berenstain Bears
and
THE TRUTH

Stan & Jan Berenstain

Random House 🏠 New York

It was a lazy sort of day in Bear Country.
The air was so still that the leaves on
the big tree house where the Bear family
lived were hardly rustling.

Except in the beehive, where the bees
were always busy, nothing much seemed
to be happening.

It was the sort of day that sometimes
leads to mischief.

Inside the tree house Brother and Sister
Bear were sitting around not doing anything
in particular.

Brother was holding his soccer ball—he'd
become interested in soccer and had been outside
practicing free kicks. Sister was relaxing in
an easy chair, thinking about what to do next.

Neither Papa nor Mama Bear was around. Papa was in his shop working on some furniture, and Mama was out shopping.

"I know what," said Sister. "Let's go gather some wild blackberries."

Brother thought about that.

"No," he said, "wild blackberries have too many thorns, and besides, the seeds get stuck in your teeth."

"Well, then," said Sister, "let's go out and twist each other up on the swing and see who gets the dizziest."

Brother thought about that.

"No," he said. "That's silly, and besides, we did that yesterday."

Sister became irritated and impatient with her brother.

"My goodness!" she complained.
"You don't want to do *anything*. All
you want to do is sit there and hug
that soccer ball. I think you must
be in love with that soccer ball!"

"I am not!" protested Brother.
"But I'll tell you something—I bet
I can dribble this ball past you!"

Brother was a pretty good soccer player
and a *very* good dribbler. But so was Sister.

The only one who saw what happened next, besides the cubs, was a mocking-bird who was perched on a twig outside an open window.

Brother faced Sister. The ball was on the floor between them. First Brother moved the ball with his right foot,

then with his left, trying to trick Sister out of position.

Then, quick as a flash, he gave the ball a sharp kick with his right.

It almost worked.

But Sister was fast too. She reached
out with her knee and blocked the ball,

which bounced against a bookshelf,

against a chair,

against a footstool,

and into Mama's *most favorite* lamp,

which fell to the floor with a crash!

The mockingbird let out a screech and got out of there as fast as its wings could carry it. As it flew away it saw Mama Bear returning from the marketplace!

Now, the Bear family had some house rules just as any family has. One was "No honey eating in bed." Another was "No tracking mud on the clean floors." And another was *"No ball playing in the house"*!

What to do? Brother looked at Sister. Sister looked at Brother. They both looked at the broken lamp. And they both listened in horror as Mama came up the front steps and into the house.

All Brother had time to do before Mama came into the room was roll the ball behind Papa's chair.

"My lamp!" said Mama. "My best lamp! What happened?" she asked, looking into her cubs' eyes. "Tell me about it."

The cubs looked into Mama's eyes, then at each other, and then they began to tell one of the biggest whoppers that has ever been told in Bear Country.

"It was a bird!" began Brother.
"Yes," added Sister, "a big purple
bird with yellow feet!"

"And green wing tips,"
added Brother.

"And funny-looking red
feathers sticking out of its
head," said Sister, as a
finishing touch.

As most lies do, the purple bird
whopper got bigger and bigger and bigger.

"Yes," continued the cubs, "and it flew in that window, zoomed around the room, and knocked over the lamp!"

As Mama Bear was looking at the broken lamp with a sad expression on her face, Papa Bear came in from his shop.

The cubs began to tell him the story of the big bird that flew in the window and broke the lamp. It was harder to tell the second time. For one thing, they couldn't quite remember how they had told it the first time.

"You've got me confused," said Papa. "Was it a purple bird with green wing tips and yellow feet?

"Or a yellow bird with purple wing tips and green feet?

"*Or* . . . was it a white bird with black spots . . .

like that soccer ball behind my easy chair?"

But the thing that really made it hard the second time was how very sad Mama looked as she picked up the pieces of the broken lamp.

"Mama, we're really sorry about the lamp," said Brother.

"Oh, yes!" said Sister, picking up the last piece and putting it in the dust pan.

"Oh," said Mama, "I'm not worried about the lamp. We can always get another lamp, or we can glue this one back together. What I'm sad about is the thought that maybe, just maybe, my cubs, whom I've always trusted, aren't telling me the truth. And trust is not something you can put back together again."

Both cubs started to talk at once.
"It wasn't a bird!" said Sister. "It was a soccer ball."
"And it was all my fault!" shouted Brother.
"It was just as much my fault!" shouted Sister.

But they were both shouted down by the phone, which rang loudly.

It was Grizzly Gran inviting the Bear family for a Sunday visit.

"Hello, Gran!" said Mama. "Oh, everything is just fine here in the tree house. How is everything with you?"

"But, Mama!" protested Sister after Mama hung up the phone. "You told Gran that everything is fine here, and that isn't really the truth."

"Oh, but it is," answered Mama. "We've got two fine cubs who have just learned a very important lesson about telling the truth. And what could be finer than that?

"Now, let's help Papa glue the lamp back together."

Nobody really expects cubs to be perfect, and from time to time Brother and Sister Bear did forget the rules.

Brother ate honey in bed a couple of times.

One time Sister tracked a little mud on the clean floor.

And once or twice Brother and Sister started to play
ball in the house before they remembered not to.

But they never, ever again told a whopper . . .

because trust is one thing you can't put back
together once it's broken.

The Berenstain Bears
FORGET THEIR MANNERS

Etiquette for Bears

"Please" and "Thank you"
Help quite a lot
To make a polite bear
Out of one who is not.

A First Time Book®

The Berenstain Bears
FORGET THEIR
MANNERS

Stan & Jan Berenstain

There was trouble in the big tree house down a sunny dirt road deep in Bear Country—trouble with manners. The Bear family's trouble with manners was that they *forgot* them!

At first it was just an occasional "please" or "thank you" that was forgotten.

Then there was a rude push without an "excuse me."

Then a reach across the table instead
of a "please pass the broccoli."

Mama Bear wasn't quite sure how or why it happened. But she was sure of one thing—whatever the reason, the Bear family had become a pushing, shoving, name-calling, ill-mannered mess!

At the table it was even worse. They were
a grabbing, mouth-stuffing, food-fighting,
kicking-under-the-table super mess!

Of course, Mama Bear tried to correct Brother and Sister Bear's behavior.

She tried coaxing.

She tried complaining.

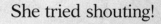

She tried shouting!

She tried going to Papa for help (though it sometimes seemed to Mama that he was part of the problem).

Papa banged on the table and shouted as only he could shout. But nothing really seemed to do any good.

Mama didn't like what was happening to her family. Not one bit. Something had to be done. But what? The best way to fight *bad* habits, she thought, was with *good* habits. Then she thought of a plan. She got a big piece of cardboard and a marker. At the top she wrote:

THE BEAR FAMILY POLITENESS PLAN

When the plan was finished,
she called a family meeting and
showed it to Papa and the cubs.

It certainly got the Bear family's attention!

THE BEAR FAMILY POLITENESS PLAN

RUDENESS	PENALTY
FORGETTING "PLEASE" OR "THANK YOU" ...	SWEEP FRONT STEPS
PUSHING OR SHOVING	BEAT 2 RUGS
INTERRUPTING ...	DUST DOWNSTAIRS
NAME CALLING ...	CLEAN CELLAR
REACHING AT TABLE	CLEAN YARD
PLAYING WITH FOOD	WASH DISHES
RUDE NOISES ...	WEED GARDEN
BANGING DOOR ...	CLEAN ATTIC
FORGETTING "EXCUSE ME" ...	EMPTY GARBAGE
HOGGING BATHROOM	PUT OUT TRASH

Mama's plan had a list of all the rude things she wanted to stop. Beside each one was a penalty—a job or chore that went with it. If you forgot a "please" or a "thank you," you had to sweep the front steps. If you pushed or shoved, you had to beat two rugs. If you got caught name calling, you had to clean the whole cellar!

"But, Mama!" sputtered the cubs. "You're not being fair!"

"It seems to me," she said, "that *you're* the ones who aren't being fair—to yourselves or anyone else. That's what manners are all about—being fair and considerate. Manners are very important. They help us get along with each other. Why, without manners—"

"Your mama's absolutely right!" interrupted Papa.

"Thank you, Papa, for your comment. But interrupting is number three on the Rude List, and the penalty is dusting the downstairs," Mama said, and handed him the feather duster.

"Hmm," said Brother. "This looks serious. I think we'd better come up with a plan of our own or we're going to be doing a lot of extra chores."

"What sort of plan?" asked Sister.

"Well," he said, "instead of just being polite, we'll be *super* polite. We'll 'please' and 'thank you' so much that Mama will get fed up and call the whole thing off!"

"Yes," said Sister. "We'll be so polite, she won't be able to stand it!"

They put their plan into action.
They were super polite . . .

—on the stairs:
  "After you, Sister dear!"
  "Thank you, dear Brother!"

—in the hall:
  "Excuse me, Brother dear!"
  "Why, certainly, my dear Sister!"

—waiting for the
bathroom:

"Terribly sorry to have
kept you waiting!"

"Think nothing of it,
my dear!"

But it didn't work the way they expected. Mama didn't get fed up at all. And after a while Brother and Sister forgot about being super polite and were just polite . . .

—at the table:
"Pass the honey, please."
"Certainly."

—in their room:
"Would you like me to help you pick up your toys?"
"Thank you very much."

—in the yard:

"Oops! Sorry—I didn't mean to bump you."

"That's all right. No harm done."

And it turned out that Mama had been right: things *did* go more smoothly. Once they got into the good manners habit, they didn't even have to think about it.

But it wasn't so easy for Papa. He was the one who got fed up. It's a little harder to change habits when you're older, and he had to do quite a few extra chores for forgetting his manners.

"I'm glad to get out of the house, away from that Politeness Plan!" he said as he drove the family along the highway on a trip to the supermarket.

"Manners and courtesy are just as important away from home—especially on the road," said Mama as they stopped at a stop sign to let pedestrians and other cars pass. "They help us drive safely."

"Well," grumbled Papa as they all went into the busy supermarket, "I think you can have too much of a good thing—you've got to have common sense along with manners! Why, if you let everyone go ahead of you at the checkout, you'd be there forever!

"And sometimes you *have* to interrupt—Excuse me, madam," he interrupted a shopper, "but I believe you have a leaking bottle in your cart!" The shopper thanked him for his help.

"You see?" he said, driving home. "There's more to life than remembering your manners. Besides, manners are all right for cubs and mama bears . . .

BONK!

"...but we papa bears have other things to think about—" At that moment the car in front stopped suddenly and Papa bumped into it. He was furious. "Why, that pinheaded fiddlebrain!" he snarled.

"Name calling!" reminded Sister.

The penalty for name calling was cleaning the whole cellar, so Papa gritted his teeth and remembered his manners. And a good thing, too. Because climbing out of the other car was the biggest, angriest bear he had ever seen!

But when the angry bear saw how polite Papa was, he remembered his manners too. He explained that he had stopped short because a mama duck and her ducklings had crossed in front of him. Then he and Papa Bear looked at their bumpers and saw that no harm had been done.

"As I was saying," said Papa as they
continued on their way, "it's very
important for us to remember our manners
at all times—and I want to thank you,
Sister, for reminding me to remember
mine."

"You're very welcome, I'm sure,"
said Sister Bear politely.

The Berenstain Bears
GET THE GIMMIES

When a cub's behavior
takes a turn for the worst,
it's hard for parents
to know what to do first.

A First Time Book®

The Berenstain Bears
GET THE GIMMIES

Stan & Jan Berenstain

Of course, the members of the Bear family, who lived in the big tree house down a sunny dirt road in Bear Country, loved each other. They loved each other very much. Brother and Sister Bear loved their mama and papa. Naturally, Mama and Papa Bear loved their cubs, and, of course, they were nice to them— as nice as they could be.

But sometimes, *sometimes* they were a little too nice. Sometimes the cubs got too many treats, too many toys, and too many rides on the Bucking Duck at the mall.

Maybe that's why Brother and Sister Bear got the gimmies. Or maybe it was because there were treats, toys, and fun things to do wherever they looked—at the supermarket, at the mall, on TV, and just about every which-where.

Maybe that was why they began making a fuss to get what they wanted—especially at the supermarket checkout, where there were always stacks and stacks of candy and other goodies.

"Now, cubs," Mama Bear said as the family got into the checkout line and she saw that old gimmie gleam in their eyes, "we can't have a big fuss every time we pass candy. I simply won't stand for it."

"But, Mama," whined Sister. "They have Gummy Gumballs! My favorite!"

"And Chewy Chompers! *My* favorite!" whined Brother.

"Now, hush!" said Mama. "I simply won't listen to another word..."

That's when Papa Bear smiled and said, "Now, Mama, you're only young once," and handed the cubs their favorite treats.

"It's only too true," said Mama as they were leaving the supermarket, "that you're only young once. But that's all the more reason to learn proper behavior while you're still young, and I certainly think—"

"Look! Look!" shouted Sister. "A new ride!"

"Hey, a Bucking Frog!" shouted Brother. "That looks even better than the Bucking Duck! May we ride it, please? May we? May we? Please!"

Now, Papa had just bought them treats, and he thought that was enough for one day. But the cubs made such a fuss that he sighed, dug into his pocket, and put some money in the slot.

Papa looked at Mama and shrugged. "Cubs will be cubs," he said.

"It may be true that cubs will be cubs," said Mama as they walked across the parking lot to their car. "But that's no excuse for jumping up and down and making a scene every time they see something they want—"

"Look! Look!" shouted the cubs once again. "Little rubber cats that stick out their tongues when you squeeze them!"

"Cubs," said Mama, "that will be quite enough! I don't want to hear another word..."

"Oh please!" they shouted. "May we have them? Please! Please! Please!" Papa decided it was time to put a stop to all the fussing.

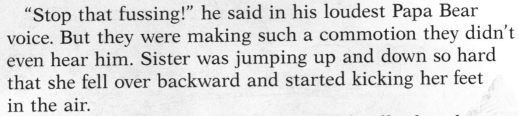

"Stop that fussing!" he said in his loudest Papa Bear voice. But they were making such a commotion they didn't even hear him. Sister was jumping up and down so hard that she fell over backward and started kicking her feet in the air.

"Please! Please!" shouted the cubs so loudly that the whole parking lot took notice.

"Er—" said embarrassed Papa to the toy seller, "two of those rubber pussycats, please."

The rubber pussycats not
only stuck out their tongues
when you squeezed them, they
went squeak-squeak as well.
And they squeak-squeaked
all the way home.

Mama was quite annoyed by the time they got back to the tree house, but Papa was so angry he could hardly speak. It wasn't until the cubs had gone about their business and Mama had made a pot of tea that Papa's voice came back loud and clear.

"Of all the outrageous, disgraceful, *embarrassing* behavior I have ever seen," he roared, "that selfish, greedy performance by our cubs was the worst! Brother and Sister have the worst case of the galloping greedy gimmies I've ever seen!"

"Yes," said Mama, calmly sipping her tea. "But have you ever stopped to think about *why* they have the gimmies? Perhaps their greedy behavior isn't all their fault. Perhaps it's partly our fault for giving in every time they make a fuss."

Papa listened quietly. "Perhaps so," he said.

"It's up to us," she continued, "to explain things to them—to help them understand why it's important not to be greedy."

Then Papa called the cubs in for a talking-to. He told them why it wasn't a good idea to be selfish and greedy and want everything in sight.

"Selfish, greedy cubs," he explained, "can never be happy, because you just can't have everything you want all the time—life isn't like that. Do you understand?"

"Oh yes, Papa. We understand," they said.

He talked to them about "counting their blessings," which meant enjoying the things they had instead of forever wanting more and more and more.

"Does that make sense to you?" he asked.

"Oh yes, Papa," they said. "It makes a lot of sense."

That's when the cubs heard the sound of a familiar car door. It was Grizzly Gramps and Gran come to call.

Brother and Sister ran to open the front door, and as Gramps and Gran came up the steps, they made the biggest fuss yet.

"Whaja-bringme?" they screamed. "Whaja-bringme? Whaja-bringme?!" That did it.

"Up to your room!" roared Papa. "Up to your room and no TV or treats for a week! For a *month*! For a *year*!"

The cubs knew this wasn't the time to argue. They scurried up the stairs and into their room.

"We seem to have come at a bad time!" said Gran.
"What about these things we brought with us?" asked
Gramps. "A puzzle for Brother and a top for Sister?"
"Your presents will have to wait, Gramps,"
answered Mama. "I'm afraid Brother and Sister
have a bad case of the gimmies."
"The *galloping greedy* gimmies,"
added Papa. "The worst case I've
ever seen."

The cubs opened their
door a crack to listen.

"The worst case, ya say?" said Gramps, looking Papa in the eye. "Seems to me you were quite a gimmie-cub yourself when you were little."

Brother and Sister sneaked to the top of the stairs so they could hear better.

"I was?" said Papa.

RUFE GRIZZLY'S GENERAL STORE

"Of course, we didn't have malls or supermarkets back then. But there was old Rufe Grizzly's General Store. Wonderful place. Sold just about everything— honey cake, licorice sticks, molasses apples, and all sorts of toys and novelties. And did you ever have the gimmies! Did you ever! You wanted everything in sight. Downright embarrassing. Why, it got so bad we couldn't go there anymore."

"So we worked out a deal," said Gran. "When it came time for a trip to the General Store, we had you decide on a treat ahead of time. It could be a sweet, a toy, or a book—and that was it for the day."

"Right," said Gramps. "And if you came down with the gimmies, we went right home and you got *nothing*!"

"That sounds like a pretty good plan to me," said Mama.

"Me too," said Papa.

The cubs tiptoed back to their
room. It sounded okay to them, too.

The next time the Bear family went to the supermarket, they tried the Gramps-and-Gran plan. And it worked!

Brother decided he would get a book about dinosaurs, and Sister wanted a new box of crayons.

Mama and Papa were very proud when the cubs passed the candy rack without so much as a peep. Brother and Sister were pretty proud of themselves, too.

But then they heard it: the familiar sound of a cub with a bad case of the gimmies. The kicking, screaming cub was just behind them in the checkout line. You never *heard* such a fuss.

"What outrageous, disgraceful, embarrassing behavior!" said Sister. *"May we leave?"*

"Yeah," said Brother. "Let's get out of here."

And that's how Brother and Sister
Bear got rid of a pretty bad case
of the galloping greedy gimmies.

The Berenstain Bears
DOLLAR$
AND
ENE

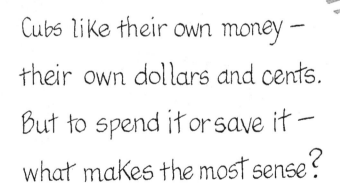

Cubs like their own money —
their own dollars and cents.
But to spend it or save it —
what makes the most sense?

A First Time Book®

The Berenstain Bears
DOLLARS AND ENE

Stan & Jan Berenstain

Money wasn't a big problem in the Bear family's tree house down a sunny dirt road deep in Bear Country. But it *was* a problem—at least where cubs Brother and Sister were concerned. They knew some things about money. They knew that Papa wasn't made of it, that it didn't grow on trees, and that they should save it for a rainy day. Papa had told them those things many times. What they didn't know about money was how to manage it.

The cubs liked money. They had liked it
even before they knew you could buy things
with it. They liked coins better than paper
money because you could do things with coins.

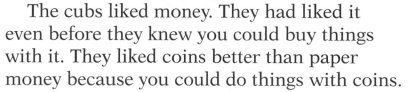

They liked to roll them.

They liked to spin them.

They liked to stack them.

As they got a little older, they liked to play "heads or tails" with them.

But by keeping their eyes and ears open at the supermarket, the hardware store, and the clothing store, they soon learned that you could do a lot more with money than just play with it. You could *buy* things with it.

You could buy all sorts of things.

Ice cream from the Good Humor Bear,

rides on the Bucking Duck at the mall,

balloons from the
balloon bear at the park.

As time went on, the cubs learned more about money. They learned the difference between the dollar sign, which was an "S" with two lines through it, and the cent sign, which was a "C" with one line through it.

"Baseball cards? Wedding dress?" shouted Papa. "You must think I'm made of money. You must think money grows on trees!" The cubs backed away. All they wanted was some green money. All they got was Papa red in the face.

Mama had been watching. She knew it was time to calm things down, and she had an idea how to do it.

"If you cubs will excuse us," she said, "there are some things I'd like to discuss with your papa."

"My dear," said Mama, "it's not going to do any good to shout at the cubs. It's as much our fault as it is theirs that they don't understand about money. It's up to us to teach them how to manage money."

"But *how*?" asked Papa.

"I suggest that we begin giving them a regular weekly allowance," she said.

"Hmm," said Papa. "That's an interesting idea. Then perhaps they will learn to be more responsible about money."

"An allowance?" said Sister.

"What's an allowance?" asked Brother.

"An allowance," said Papa, "is a sum of money that you will get at the beginning of every week. It will be up to you to manage it—to spend it or save it as you see fit."

"Hmm," said Papa.
"Double hmm,"
said Mama.

When the cubs returned,
they each had a pile of
candy bars, bubble gum,
and trading cards.

They had spent their whole allowance on the first day of the week.

And they did the same thing the next week,

and the next,

and the next.

It was clear to Mama and Papa that the allowance idea wasn't working as planned, and it certainly wasn't teaching the cubs how to manage money.

The cubs would quickly eat the candy bars and get tired of the other things they bought. Then they would mope and groan because they didn't have any money left for the rest of the week.

"Mama," said Brother. "I don't think this allowance idea is working out."

"I quite agree," said Mama. "But what do you suggest?"

"*A bigger allowance!*" said the cubs as one.

"Possibly," said Mama. "But that is something we'll have to discuss with your papa."

"Well, let's discuss it with him right now," said Sister.

"Oh, no," said Mama. "Papa is balancing the checkbook. I never interrupt your papa while he's balancing the checkbook."

Hmm. Checkbook, thought Mama. Our checkbook helps Papa and me manage *our* money. It gives us a chance to think about how we should spend it. It gives us a record of how much money we have spent and how much we have left.

Mama went into the kitchen. She rummaged around in the cupboard drawer. It was filled with things she wasn't quite ready to throw away. Among the things were some extra checkbooks that were left over from when she changed banks. But how to explain the idea of checks and checkbooks to the cubs, she wondered.

Mama told Papa what she had in mind. Then she explained the idea of checks to the cubs.

"Do you mean you're taking *away* our allowances?" protested Brother.

"Not at all," said Papa. "As a matter of fact, we're increasing your allowances. But instead of giving them to you at the beginning of each week so that you can go out and spend them before they burn a hole in your pockets, we're going to hold them for you. Then when you want a little pocket money or want to buy something, you write out a check.

"Here, I'll show you how it's done.

"First you make it out to 'Cash,' like so. Then you put how much it's for—in words as well as numbers so there can't be any mistake. Then you write what it's for on this line and sign it at the bottom and on the back. Then you give it to Mama and she gives you the money and keeps a record. It's that simple."

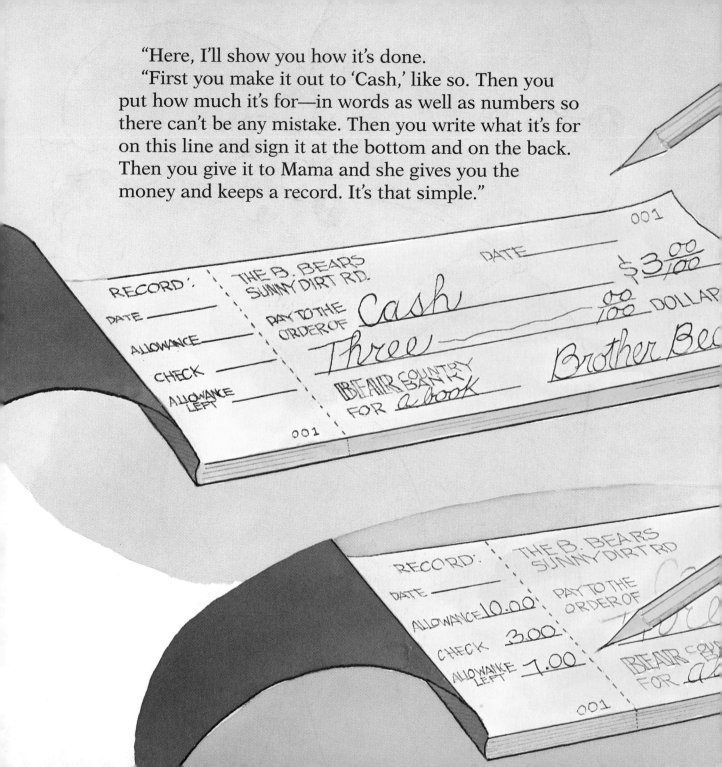

Brother got the idea right away and gave Mama the check for three dollars, and she gave him the cash. He changed his mind about spending five dollars (half his allowance) on baseball cards and bought a baseball book instead. Sister changed her mind, too. She decided to save her first week's allowance and buy the Bearbie wedding dress with her *next* week's allowance so she would still have ten dollars left.

"Now, that's what I call *money managing*,"
said Mama to Papa.

Available in stores September 2002

Attention, fans of the Berenstain Bears!
Get ready to take the trip of a lifetime. . . .

Did you know that Stan and Jan Berenstain were both art directors of their high school yearbooks?

Did you know that the first book featuring the Bear family was called *The Big Honey Hunt*?

Did you know that the man who commissioned that fateful book was none other than Theodor Geisel, otherwise known as Dr. Seuss?

Find out the fascinating details of the lives and careers of Stan and Jan, the inspired husband-and-wife team who created America's first ursine family— the beloved Berenstain Bears.

Title: DOWN A SUNNY DIRT ROAD
Authors: Stan & Jan Berenstain
Format: Jacketed hardcover
With photos and original art
ISBN: 0-375-81403-5
Price: $20.00 U.S. / $30.00 CAN.
Pages: 208
Grade Range: Grades 7 & up
Also available in Gibraltar Library Binding.

If you're a fan of the Berenstain Bears First Time Books® . . .
then you'll *love* these Berenstain Bears early readers!

0-679-88717-2

0-679-89225-7

0-679-88720-2

0-679-89226-5

0-679-88718-0

0-679-88719-9

0-679-89227-3

0-679-89230-3

0-679-89229-X

0-679-89228-1

Step into a whole new Berenstain Bears experience
with books you can read all on your own!
From the Step into Reading® series at Random House.

These Step into Reading® titles starring the Berenstain Bears are a natural fit
for beginning readers who've grown up with—and grown to love!—the Bear family.
The simple text and engaging art are a perfect fit for them as they gain confidence
and enthusiasm about reading—key ingredients for a lifetime of reading success!